I0780642

A Dragon for Christmas

M.D. Neu

Copyright © 2017, 2025 by M.D. Neu

All rights reserved.

No part of this book may be reproduced or transmitted in any form or by any means, electronic or mechanical, except for the purpose of review and/or reference, without explicit permission in writing from the publisher.

Cover design copyright © 2025 by Niki Lenhart
nikilen-designs.com

Published by Water Dragon Publishing
waterdragonpublishing.com

Experience our other Dragon Gems titles
waterdragonpublishing.com/dragon-gems

ISBN 978-1-969655-06-7 (Trade Paperback)

10 9 8 7 6 5 4 3 2 1

For my niece Breanne, who inspired Carmen and my sister Dawn who is now and always been Rella.

Acknowledgements

THIS STORY would not have been possible without my friends and fellow writers over at Scribophile. You've helped me grow and taught me more about writing and story craft than any class or book ever could.

A big thank you to my editor, Jason.

Lastly, I have to thank my partner and husband Eric for all his support, without him none of this would be possible.

A Dragon for Christmas

1

"**C**ARMEN, *MIJA,* YOU AWAKE? Do you want something to eat?"

I open my eyes. "I'm not hungry."

"You need to eat. How do you expect to keep your strength?"

I don't respond. The magical charms upset my stomach to the point where I can't eat. I know they are supposed to fight the curse, but do they have to make me feel so bad? Even the ones my dad helps to create. They all suck.

"*Mija?*"

"I'll eat something later, I promise." I have to respond, or Mom'll keep bugging me. All I want to do is rest.

I glance out the window to the training yard. This year, I'm getting my dragon for Christmas, and I'll have different charms that hopefully won't make me feel crummy all the time. That'll be good. I thought I was going to get it a few years ago when Mattie got hers, but my bonding with the Yellow-Tip Dragon didn't stick even with the fancy charms the Master Dragon Trainer created.

It sucked after the Yellow-Tip was gone and I was cleared of its influence. I had to start the whole testing and training process again. It was either go through the process or have the curse come back full force, and I really didn't want that to happen.

Oh look, an African Tiger-Stripe just flew by the window.

There are all kinds of different dragons that people can get, like the California Green Belly—that's what Mattie has. I'm hoping for the Blue Bottom from Lake Tahoe or the Mountain Poppy—it's a pretty orange. I suppose I shouldn't be picky as long as I get a dragon. I have to remind myself not everyone can get one. You have to be born special, like me. I forget the exact day, but back when I was seven, my folks and the Master Dragon Trainer told me I was going to get my very own dragon. I was so excited because I met Mattie around the same time, and I realized when we grew up I was going to marry her.

I watch the dragons flying around down in the training yard amongst the trees. Seeing the other kids playing with their dragons, I wish I could be with them. It's not cold and there isn't any rain today, but I'm stuck in my room, recovering from my last round of tests. I shift in my bed for a better view out the window, but I can't see Mattie or Gary, her dragon. She must be with her parents.

I hope she comes by. She smells like strawberries, and her smile and laugh make me feel better.

When I talk about marrying Mattie, my dad tells me to focus on my dragon first. My mom doesn't like me talking like that. I think it upsets her, but I don't get why.

When I tell the DTs (Dragon Techs) about me and Mattie, they smile and remind me I need to focus on my testing and training.

Dragon training is important, but so is being friends with Mattie. Why can't I do both at the same time? I guess it's because the training isn't easy and I get tired a lot, but if that's what it takes to get my dragon, then I'm gonna do it.

I shift again, unable to get comfortable. I've been in this room too long and need to get outside and move around. If I were at home, I'd be in my own room. My bed is huge and fluffy with lots of pillows. Mom let me pick them out myself. I love my house, it always smells like freshly baked bread. Well, it used to, before I started training for my dragon. Now it smells funny, like the training center. My mom is always cleaning and doesn't want to bake anymore.

Still, I'm lucky. I don't live far from one of the best dragon training campuses in the country, the Packard Family Dragon Foundation. It's amazing, and right next door is this big fancy college. I hope to go there when I get older, but my dad wants me to go to his school where he teaches. Anyway, I have time before I have to make that choice.

A Gilroy Glider soars by my window. It's double the size of the African Tiger-Stripe and is a solid brown color. *So cool.*

There are three humungous dragon-breeding centers here as well, so I'm doubly lucky. I've gotten to go to the big facility in San Jose, where we live. It's huge and filled with at least one of every type of dragon. Mattie and I went there once during one of her extended stays at the center while she was training. We had such a blast.

Mattie's family has to come from Reno for her training. Now that she has her dragon, she only needs to come and make sure the bond is holding and ensure she and her dragon are getting along. They also check her charms to make sure they are still assisting with the dragon bond. Sometimes they need to exchange them for stronger charms.

I can't wait for that.

Mattie's dragon is red and green with big wings as long as a school bus. Most California Green Bellies have a lot of green in them and are gigantic, like the size of a car. I bet Mattie will be able to fly on Gary if she wants to, someday when he's full-grown. Gary started out tiny and all green, but now when I see him, he's mostly red, but he still has his green belly, which has tiny little hairs that make it fuzzy and soft.

According to this book I read on dragons, the California Green Belly used to spit fire, but that trait was bred out of them a long time ago. That kinda sucks because a fire-breathing dragon would be so cool.

Gary and Mattie seem to get along. And I guess it's good he doesn't breathe fire. I wouldn't want anything to happen to Mattie or me. I've gotten to go out with them in the yard a few times during their training sessions. He's amazing. And makes me want my own dragon even more.

I've got the name of my dragon picked out, but I'm not supposed to say yet, so I don't.

My dragon, when I get her, I'm sure is going to be a Blue Bottom with a purple body and long blue wings.

She's going to have a sleek fast body, not big and bulky like Gary.

I cough.

"You okay, *mija*?" my mom asks from behind her tablet, brown eyes narrowing. Her black hair is brushed back in a ponytail, and I think she has perfect eyebrows.

She and Dad are here most days. This last session was really hard on me, but I pulled through and the new charms seem to have helped with the curse, even with the loss of appetite it caused. When I woke up the other day, they were both in my room, watching me. Now whenever I move or cough, my mom asks if I'm all right.

Ugh.

"I'm fine. Just tired of being in bed."

"Later, we can take you out to the yard. If you promise to eat something."

I nod.

My mom goes back to her tablet.

I suppose I shouldn't complain. My mom works for a high-tech company that gave her a lot of time off for my training. My dad is a professor of Spellcraft and Mysticism at Santa Clara University. Magic runs on his side of the family, so he got a job teaching it to others. He's been doing it forever, although the only spells I've seen him conjure are charms. I guess his job is important because the Master Dragon Trainer and he talk a lot, especially about my charms. I heard he's good at removing curses, but my parents want me to focus on the dragon, so I don't hear a lot. Especially these days with how sick I've been.

I wonder if my family being magical is part of the reason curses affect me the way they do. I'm not sure, because Mattie's parents aren't magical, so I don't know.

I'm sore. I hate all the testing; it takes so long. Months sometimes. At least I get to decorate my room the way I want and I don't get stuck sharing. That's good. I wouldn't mind sharing with Mattie, but she gets to stay in a different part of the campus.

On my wall are a bunch of posters of dragons and a few of my favorite movies. Oh, and I love Lady Gaga and Beyoncé. Right now, they are my faves, and I have them both on my wall across from me where I can stare at them. At least when I'm not studying or watching TV.

I huff and play with the long strands of my hair as I look out at the training grounds. There are so many people out there today with their dragons. I bet the puffy white clouds make it all smell fresh like rain. I miss that smell. When I'm testing, I don't get to go out in the rain like I used to, not until I'm healthy.

The African Tiger-Stripe lands on a dragon perch outside my window. Our gazes meet and my stomach jumps with excitement. In a month, I'm going to have one. I'm going to have to train my dragon and take care of her. I'll get to be outside again.

"Carmen, you okay?" my mom glances at me again.

"I'm just looking out at the yard. I'm trying to figure out the kind of dragon I want."

Mom smiles at me. "You know, you don't always get to pick. Sometimes, they pick you. Remember what happened last time."

I nod.

Last time, I didn't have a choice and I ended up with this pretty Yellow-Tip Dragon. It was so tiny, about the size of my hand. He and I didn't bond, so when he was just about my size, maybe a month later, he left and I had to start the process all over again. That was a bummer, and everyone was upset and worried. Even though they didn't say anything. I figured it out.

Dragons are the ultimate protection for kids like me from curses, and we protect them. They have to stay with us our entire lives once we bond because we are completely dependent on each other. That's why we need the charms and all the testing. Sometimes I wonder what it would be like not to be a Dragon Keeper, but if that happened, I would never have met Mattie. Anyway, the process of getting a dragon is hard, and they don't always stay. You have to really be lucky and get the right one.

"I want a Blue Bottom." I turn to my mom.

She chuckles. "You'll have to wait and see what the Master Trainers come up with. You know how hard the process is."

"I know, Mom."

The small frown on her lips vanishes before I can really comment.

"I just hope my dragon and Gary get along. Blue Bottoms and California Green Bellies are supposed to get along really well, but not always, so I hope they do. They're gonna have to be friends if me and Mattie are gonna be married."

"Carmen, don't talk like that ..."

I cross my arms over my chest. Sometimes, I want to yell at her, but I don't.

"You're too young to know who you're going to marry."

I turn from my mom. She thinks because I'm only eleven, I don't know stuff, but I do. I understand that she and Dad work really hard so I can train. I overheard that she had to ask for money from my *abuelo* to pay for my testing. Sometimes, she cries because she is so worried about me, and Dad has to sit with her and tell her I'm at one of the best training facilities in the world and it won't be like the last time with the Yellow-Tip. See, I know stuff and it's fine.

I smile, thinking about my wedding day. We'll have a big party. Mattie will be in a pretty dress that matches Gary, all reds and greens. I'm gonna be in blues and purples, matching my dragon. There will be music and all kinds of good food. With my aunties' tamales and my mom's pupusas; it's gonna be so beautiful.

"Honey, do you have your list for Santa?"

Santa? Really? But who am I to say anything different to my mom?

"I don't need anything, Mom. Just my dragon." I don't want to ask for anything more because the dragon is gonna be a lot and all the training and follow-up that goes with it. Mattie and I talk about this stuff when our parents aren't around. Mattie will sit on my bed, and we laugh and talk. Sometimes, she'll hold my hand and I get all tingly. It's nice.

"Carmen, come on. Santa needs to bring you something. Especially since you'll be here at the testing facility. Maybe you should ask for your own cell phone."

"Really?" I turn to my mom. Is she serious? A phone of my own? That would be great. "You mean it? You think I'll get one?"

I could text Mattie all the time if I had my own.

"Well, you have to ask Santa. I can't say for sure," she said over the top of her tablet. "Maybe you haven't been good enough this year."

"That would be so cool." I lean back on my pillow, allowing the softness to engulf me. Mattie has her own phone because she's a year older than me, but I get to use my mom's when I want. Still, having my own personal cell would be great.

The door to my room opens, revealing Mattie, the bright lights illuminating her like an angel.

"Hi, Mrs. Garcia," Mattie says as the door closes.

"Hi, Mattie." My mom puts down her tablet. "How are you feeling today?"

"I'm good. No side effects from my training or the charms, so I'll get to go home after Christmas."

"That's wonderful news." Mom smiles.

"Hey, Carmen." Mattie rushes over. She has bright blue eyes and beautiful brown hair that she brushes back in a ponytail. She wears glasses, but they make her look so pretty.

"Hi." I wave and sit up higher in my bed.

"How was your testing?" Mattie pulls the chair from the corner over to my bed.

"The DTs say it went good. I'm just tired."

"I remember. The testing is the worst."

"Where's Gary?"

Mattie points to the window. Outside is her big red-and-green dragon. He's sitting on a dragon perch. He puffs out some smoke and shakes his wings at me to say hi.

"He's getting huge!"

Mattie nods. "My folks worry he'll be too big. But it would be cool to ride on his back." She glances over at him. "He's still too small and not strong enough to carry his weight and mine."

"Bummer. Still, riding him would be amazing."

"The Master Dragon Trainer said our bonding is going really well and that I won't need to come back for two months, when they check out my charms." She holds up two fingers.

"Lucky." I try not to frown. I want to be happy for Mattie and Gary, but that means I won't get to see her as often and that sucks. Now I really hope I get a phone from Santa.

"Mattie, *mija*, did both your parents come this trip?" my mom asks.

"Yes, ma'am."

My mom slips her tablet in her bag. "Can I trust you two alone? I want to go talk to your folks."

I laugh. "Nah, we're gonna jump on Gary's back and fly away."

Mattie laughs.

I love that bubbly laugh.

My mom purses her lips and points at me. "Remember, Santa is watching."

"Yes, Mom."

Mattie and I watch as my mom head out the door. The door clicks behind her.

"Santa?" Mattie gets up from the chair and jumps on the bed, sitting with her legs crisscrossed. I get a whiff of her strawberry scent.

"As long as I believe in Santa, I get gifts." I adjust my legs so Mattie has more room.

"Are you excited about getting your dragon?"

I try to hide my frown, but I don't think I'm fast enough.

"What?" Mattie's eyes narrow on me. "Carmen, what's wrong?"

"What if she doesn't like me? What if she goes away like the Yellow-Tip did?"

"That won't happen. You're older. Last time, you were seven. That was too young. Even the Master Dragon Trainer said the chances of the Yellow-Tip sticking around weren't very good."

"I just ..." I pull at the strings of my blanket, which I suddenly find so fascinating. "The training costs so much and I heard my folks talking about selling the house to pay for more training if this doesn't work. I don't want to move if it doesn't happen this time. Maybe I don't really need a dragon to protect me from curses."

I want to add that I'm getting tired of trying, but I keep that to myself.

"Carmen, it'll work."

"How do you know?"

"Gary told me."

Gary shakes his head back and forth, and his muzzle dips in agreement.

"What if I end up like Jasper? His parents spent all that time and money only for him not to end up with his dragon, and he got cursed really bad and almost died. And with no dragon of his own, the charms won't protect him for so long." I finally get the string loose and pull it from the blanket.

"That's not gonna happen."

"You don't know."

Mattie nods. "Yes I do, 'cause you promised to marry me and we can't do that unless we both have dragons."

I look into her eyes and smile and nod.

Mattie always makes me feel better.

• • •

"See, I told you your mom would let you come outside with me and Gary." Mattie brushes her ponytail back over her shoulder.

"Why can't I walk? Why do I have to sit in this stupid wheelchair?" I grumble as we watch a pair of Canadian Whites chase each other, using Gary as the target to run around. I was right about the air. The clouds and the slight chill make it smell fresh and clean, even with the musty smells of the dragons.

"You know the rules. You can't overdo while you're recovering from the testing. The charms are good, but not that good. They can't keep the curse away all on their own, just temporarily." Mattie rubs a hand under Gary's muzzle as he huffs out some smoke. "He's getting annoyed at the Whites."

"Yah think?" I was getting annoyed just watching them.

"Listen, in a few more weeks you're going to go in for your final test. Once you pass, you get the charms for your dragon." Mattie smiles at me.

Gary snaps at the Whites and they scurry off.

Mattie and I laugh to the point where we both start coughing. I don't mind the coughing because it's good being out with Mattie.

"What do you think it'll be like when we get older?" I ask after we both calm down.

"We'll have a big house with plenty of room for our dragons, of course."

"Of course."

"I'm going to be a detective. I want to help people." Mattie leans back and glances up to the blue sky.

"I think I want to be a magic teacher like my dad." Dad promised to teach me after I get my dragon and come home.

"That'd be cool."

"If I do that, I'll get to bring my Blue Bottom with me to school." I laugh. "That would be so amazing. Not a lot of magic teachers have dragons."

Mattie's phone chirps, and she pulls it out of her pocket. She sighs. "It's my mom. She says we need to come back. The DTs want to check you out again."

"They suck."

"If it helps you to get your dragon, does it really matter?"

"I suppose not." I release the brakes of my wheelchair, and we head back to my room. Gary flaps his big wings behind us.

2

TODAY IS MY FINAL TEST and I'm really nervous. If everything goes well, I'll get my first set of charms that will link me to my dragon. Dad holds my hand as the DTs wheel me and my gurney down the hall to the testing center. I glance up at him. He's so tall, like really tall—about six feet. His professor robes dust the floor, but it's his hat that makes him look even taller. Strands of his brown hair peek from under the cap. We have the same brown hair. He faces me and smiles, and I see his dimples. I got those too.

Mom chats with the Master Dragon Trainer ahead of us. She's wearing jeans and a peach sweater. Her black hair bounces around her shoulders as she and the trainer talk.

Dad stops our journey and reaches into his robes. "My class has been working on this charm for you." He pulls out this little purple bag, and I get the whiff of rosemary and coffee. It kind of stinks. "I understand how important it is to you to get a Blue Bottom and you want it to be a girl just like you, so—" He tucks the bag into my hand. "—if you don't get what you want, my whole class fails, so it might be a good idea for you to make sure it happens."

"Thanks, Dad." I slip the charm bag—bad odor and all—in my pocket.

As long as I've been coming to dragon training, my dad has been making me charms. Unfortunately, magic isn't an exact science, so sometimes they don't work, but lucky for me, dad is smart and powerful so they mostly work. Well, to some degree.

"Dad?"

He squeezes my hand.

"What if a dragon doesn't pick me?"

"Carmen, the dragons have already selected you, I have to believe that," he says. "They chose you the day you were born." He gives my hand another squeeze. "Today is all about ensuring you're ready for the bonding."

"But last time ..." I glance at my feet.

He squats and takes my face in his big hands. "We pushed you too hard last time. We all knew the risks, but we thought ..." He inhaled. "You weren't ready. That's why you couldn't see your dragon, and that's why you got the Yellow-Tip. It wasn't what any of us wanted, but we hoped. I guess the dragons weren't ready for you then, but now they are."

"How do we know I'll be ready this time?"

He peeked up to Mom and then around the hall. "Do you feel ready?"

I nod.

"Can you picture your dragon? Every detail?"

I close my eyes.

Blue with purple highlights and purple eyes. She's going to have a long muzzle and sharp pointed horns at the top of her head that grow in smaller spikes down her neck to her back. Her wings are going to be huge, double her height. Her arms will end in four-fingered paws so she can hold things if she wants, or if she needs to fight. She's going to have a long sleek tail that has three spikes at the end.

"You picturing her now?"

I nod again and open my eyes.

"Do you feel ready?"

"I think ... I know I'm ready. I can feel it." I play with the ends of my long hair, twisting it in my fingers.

"That's my girl." He hugs me tight. "When you were seven and we found out you were special, your mother and I weren't sure what we were going to do. Curses are scary stuff, even with the best magic and most powerful charms. It wasn't easy for us, but we learned all there was about dragons and I know, deep down, you're going to be the best Dragon Keeper out there."

"You sure?"

"Of course. You're my daughter, and you can do anything you want."

"Even marry Mattie?" I figured I would push how far his support would go since he was being so supportive.

"If that's what you and Mattie want, then your mother and I will be there and we'll have the biggest and best wedding for the two of you possible."

I wrap my arms as much as I can around Dad.

"I hope you're saving a hug or two for me." Mom says.

"We are," Dad says.

My mom pulls me and Dad tight. All three of us are quiet for a bit, but finally Mom whispers, "You ready?"

I pull back from them and nod. Suddenly, I'm scared. I want this to work so much. I want to get my dragon, and I want it to be before Christmas. According to the DTs, Christmas Dragons are even more magical and more powerful than other dragons. They say the bond at Christmas is the strongest because of all the Christmas magic in the world. I hope they're right.

The Master Dragon Trainer walks over to my gurney.

"I was talking to the Master Dragon Trainer, and everything is ready for your test." Mom smiles, but her eyes are red and that means she's been crying again.

The Master Dragon Trainer peers down to me. "Well, Carmen, this is it. You excited?"

I gulp. I wish Mattie was here with me. My parents promised that she'll be there when I'm finished. Dad even talked to Mattie's parents about it while I was there with them all. I wish she could be here now. I could do anything with Mattie by my side.

"I think she's a little worried," my dad says, not letting go of my hand.

"All your tests have been excellent. You've scored higher than 90 percent of our candidates. You're as ready as I've seen. You'll be fine," Master Dragon Trainer Baqri says. His white teeth stand out against his caramel-colored skin and short black hair.

"Will you be with me the entire time?" I ask.

Master Trainer Baqri nods. "Of course, Carmen. I'm with all my candidates during their final test as are my team of DTs. We just need you to give us the go-ahead."

I inhale and glance up at my mom and dad. I smile. "I can do this."

Dad wraps his arm around Mom's waist. "Of course you can. I've never doubted it."

"We'll see you after your test." Mom is standing there so tall and strong I really want to be like her when I grow up, even though we don't always get along.

"You've got my charm?" Dad rustles my hair.

I pull out the stinky bag and show him.

"Remember," he says with a wink, "all seventy of my students passing rely on you passing today."

I smile at him and stuff the charm back into my pocket. "I'm ready." My dad won't fail his class, but it was nice of him to say that.

My folks stand there, and the charm in my pocket begins warming up.

The DTs seem to appear from the walls and start pushing me again. We follow Master Trainer Baqri through a large set of double doors, then another set of doors into a large white room. I look around at all the testing equipment and wrap my hand around the charm.

"Carmen, what is the name of your new dragon?" Master Trainer Baqri asks.

It's all right to tell him. It's part of the rules. "Her name's gonna be Rella."

"Rella." He makes a note of something. I can hear him writing. "What kind of dragon is Rella going to be?"

"A Blue Bottom from Tahoe."

"That sounds like an amazing dragon. I want you to close your eyes and start to picture your Blue Bottom. Every detail, and let's hope your Blue Bottom named Rella hears you."

I do as I'm told, and I start to picture Rella. She's blue with purple highlights and purple eyes. She has a long muzzle and sharp pointed horns at the top of her head that grow in smaller spikes down her neck to her back. Her wings are going ...

•   •   •

I blink my eyes clear. The sky is bright blue. The air is cool and damp, and the rushing wind whistles in my ears and blows my hair back. I glance down, and I'm on the back of my fully grown dragon. She's beautiful. Every detail about her unchanged. Even down to the three fingers and thumb on each of her paws. Her eyes are the color of lilacs, and her skin is so blue it almost vanishes in the sky. Just like I pictured, her wings are purple.

I raise up my hands as we soar past a big puffy white cloud. "This is amazing."

Rella goes into a nosedive and I hold on. Her power and speed force me close to her back. Her skin is so warm. I can't believe it. This is better than anything imaginable.

I was expecting her skin to be hard and scaly, but it's soft and smooth. It moves easily under my touch.

She glances back at me and nods. I run my hand along her back and lower neck. I love this. I'm able to control her movements with simple touches. I read that as you and your dragon's bond continues to grow, you can think commands and she'll do it.

I think about home and Rella banks to the east towards my distant neighborhood. We get real low to the trees. Everything is decorated for Christmas. All the Christmas lights and the displays in people's yards. Up ahead I see my house. There aren't any lights up, and I don't see the tree in the front window. I guess my parents didn't want to do anything this year with me at dragon training.

Next year, I'm gonna help, and we're gonna have a big tree with lots of presents and more lights on the house than anyone else. Rella huffs and I rub her neck. "Right, girl? Next Christmas is gonna be huge, and we'll both be there."

Rella circles my house a few times. I get a faint scent of fresh cookies. It must be the neighbors. They always bake. I love the aroma from their house at Christmas. I hope they are going to bring us cookies this year.

I wonder if I could fly to Mattie's house from here with Rella. It's a long trip by car, but on the back of my dragon, we'd be there in no time. "I bet you could have us there in minutes." I rub Rella's neck again. She clicks her jaw, and a quake runs through her body.

Is that a dragon laugh?

"I want to see the park."

Rella's giant wings flap, and soon enough, we're downtown. It's night, and Christmas in the Park is all lit up. The big tree outside the hotel and all the carnival rides flicker like jewels in a treasure box. It's so pretty. I haven't been down here since I was little, way before my dragon training. Mom and Dad brought me, and I got to sit on Santa's lap. I love seeing all the displays and the trees. The smells of hot cocoa fill my nose, and I get hints of cinnamon from the food vendors.

People wave to us as we fly back. I lift both my hands and pump them in the air, and people clap and cheer. Rella's neck elongates, and her wings flap, shifting up to the right then to the left.

She is showing off.

A choir sings "Silent Night" on the main stage next to the huge Christmas tree. The words and music echo off the buildings. My cheeks are aching from all my grinning. Laughter catches my ear, and I turn, which causes Rella to move in that direction, and we fly over to the ice skating rink. I want to do that when I'm finished with training. I can't wait to do all these new things once I get Rella.

As amazing as this all is, it's time to get back to the training campus. I want to fly away with Rella, find Mattie and Gary, and the four of us fly far away. That would be so amazing.

"Someday," I whisper as we head back to the campus.

3

RADUALLY, I OPEN MY EYES. My mouth tastes like a sandbox, and I can't move. As I blink my eyes, I remember flying on Rella. Totally amazing. I was free and happy, and it was the best I felt in a long time—well, since all the training and testing started. I take a deep breath and sleepily glance around. I'm back in my room. I'm not on the gurney anymore, so I must be better.

"*Mija*." My mom jumps from her chair next to my bed.

"I'm tired." I manage to say.

"The testing was harder than they thought. They had to bring in a specialist and additional equipment," Dad says. He's on the other side of my bed.

I turn to face him.

"How are you feeling? Can we get you something?"

"Did it work?" I try and shift, but my body is slow to respond. "Did I get my dragon? I don't feel any different."

I see all sorts of charms around me—some I'd never seen before and some I was unfortunately too familiar with, like the one to keep the curse away. That one always makes my stomach upset so I can't eat. I hoped never to see that particular charm again. But it's here so maybe the testing didn't work.

"We haven't been told yet." My mom hugs me.

"Where's Mattie?"

"Outside." Dad lets go of my hand. I didn't realize he was holding it. "Everyone is here. Mattie and her folks as well as your Aunt Rebecca and Uncle Joaquin and your grandparents."

"Okay," I say through a drowsy haze.

"We were worried about you." Mom lets me go. "The final test took longer than expected. The DTs and Master Trainer Baqri were with you, so we had to wait for news until you were finished."

"Did I get my dragon?" I think I asked already, but I don't remember the answer.

"*Mija*, we don't know." Mom takes my hand in hers.

I think I frown, but the side of my mouth is a little wet so I probably drool instead.

Gross.

I reach up with my other hand and wipe my mouth. I sniff and the stink of the coffee and rosemary assault my nose. I drop the charm and it lands on my lap.

They let me keep it. I thought that wasn't allowed. Something must have gone wrong.

The door creaks open and I turn my head. The light from the hall floods into my room, and standing there is the outline of Mattie. She rushes over next to my mom, stopping short of jumping on the bed.

"I saw Rella," I say.

"Rella?" Mattie asks.

"I named my dragon, Rella. After *Cinderella*, your favorite movie."

Mattie smiles. My body warms and my heart speeds up.

Mom looks at her, then over to Dad as everyone shuffles in. Both sets of grandparents are here and Aunt Rebecca and Uncle Joaquin. I never realized how small the room was until everyone piled in.

Everyone is talking so fast and my mind is moving so slow that I don't understand much of anything. My grandparents are fussing, not over me, yet, but over my mom and dad. I'm glad for the break. There are four of them and only one of me, and that's a lot of fussing. My uncle chats about how I better be getting my dragon after all this, or he is going to have a conversation with the DTs and Master Trainer. Mattie's parents are talking with my parents about the process and what to expect at this point.

Mattie pulls over a chair and takes my hand.

I give it a squeeze. It feels nice and makes all my worry and fear vanish. Still I have to ask. "Where's my dragon?" I whisper.

"It'll show up. You'll feel it."

"But the bonding." I frown. I need to start the bonding right away, and I have to get the new charms or none of it will work and I won't be protected from the curse. At least according to the books.

"But, it's almost Christmas, and it won't matter. You'll end up with the best possible bond." Mattie pats my hand.

"Mattie." I lean closer and glance over to my family who are all busy talking. "Mattie, I'm scared. What if it doesn't work? You had your dragon right away."

Mattie's gaze narrows, and for the first time in all the years we've known each other, I know she is angry, her blue eyes bore into me. "Don't you talk like that, Carmen Maria Garcia. You're going to get your dragon. We're both going to have dragons, and that's that." She squeezes my hand tight enough to make her point.

"Okay," I'm not sure I believe her, but I don't want to upset her more than I already have.

We sit there quietly, not talking, watching each other. My *abuela* comes over and stuffs my hand with a new charm. My dad's family is big on charms. This one smells like vanilla and cinnamon. As far as charms go, this one smells great. I sit there as my *abuela* says a few prayers with me, and Mattie gets pushed farther away as all the fussing begins.

The door to my room opens. I didn't think it was possible for any more people to fit, but Master Trainer Baqri strolls in. He isn't smiling, and that is never a good sign.

The room becomes so silent that I think I've lost my hearing. But it is the kind of power a Master Dragon Trainer possesses. "How are you doing, Carmen?"

"I'm tired."

He crosses the room to my bed as everyone steps out of his way. Instead of the parting of the Red Sea, it's more like the parting of the butts. I smile. At least my brain is starting to work again.

"That's to be expected," Master Trainer Baqri says. "As you can see, there is no dragon here. Now, that doesn't mean you weren't selected or that you aren't getting a dragon, so don't worry," he says that more to my mom and dad than me. Facing them. "However, we're going to keep watch and monitor you." This part he says to me. His smile doesn't reach his eyes, and I'm not sure I believe him.

"Okay." I swallow and glance over to Mattie, and she gives me a thumbs-up.

"The next ten days will be the big test. If a dragon doesn't show up by the new year, then we'll reevaluate your status and go from there, but I'm not worried." He nods. "I've already scheduled you for your charm session for the second week of January." Master Trainer Baqri pulls out his tablet and makes a few notes. "In the meantime, I want you and your family to have a great Christmas. You can get anything you want from the kitchen. The cooks are under my orders, so the sky's the limit."

My stomach grumbles. "Even pizza and ice cream?" It was nice to think about food and really want to eat and not just have to eat to keep my strength up.

"Yes, ma'am." He rests a hand on my leg. "You did amazingly well during the final test. I have no doubt everything will be fine."

"Thank you," Dad says.

"Now, I have a few other candidates to go and check on," Master Trainer Baqri slips his tablet into his long white work coat.

With each step Master Trainer Baqri takes to the door, the volume of the conversation in my room increases. Once he's gone, there is so much noise I want to put a pillow over my head to block it out. Instead, I smile at Mattie as she walks back over to my bedside.

•　　•　　•

Why my mom insists on playing Christmas music as we open presents is beyond me. There are only so many times I can hear "Frosty the Snowman," especially since San Jose has no snow, not even on the hills this year. Plus, I am not in the mood for presents. I want my dragon to show up. It has been two days and nothing. Not even Aunt Rebecca's tamales cheered me up. And I made sure to eat a bunch of them just to make sure. Instead, I sit here with a bunch of presents and out the window all I see is rain.

"Carmen, open your gifts." My dad leans over from his chair and picks up a wrapped box.

"What does it matter?"

"*Mija.*" Mom tries to keep her voice as level as possible. "I realize you wanted your dragon by Christmas ..."

I turn from her and the window. I can't watch her try to cheer me up. All I see is the red and puffiness of her eyes. She's been crying but hiding it from me.

I know it's not good. I know the curse will come back.

"What about this one from Mattie?" Dad holds up a medium flat box with a bright gold bow on it.

I sigh. I take a bite of the cookie from our neighbor. It's chocolate chip and yummy. It's not their fault. I have to be patient, but it's so hard. I saw Rella. I flew on her. So why isn't she here yet? If I miss the window to get my charms, then I have to start all over again, and that means more time feeling crummy and more money my parents have to spend to keep the curse from coming back, money I don't think they have. I don't want them to have to sell the house. Plus, I'm tired of always feeling lousy. I need my dragon.

I reach out, pick up the present, rip through the wrapping, and open the box. It's a picture in a silver frame of Mattie and me from when we first met. We were kids. Even though Mattie was older, I was taller, at least back then. Now she's taller than me. We are both out in the dragon training yard, wearing dumb Christmas hats because we had to shave our heads for the first part of our testing. I run a hand along the frame. That was a bad Christmas. We were both sick because of the charms and the curse, and the training was awful. This was probably our best day that whole holiday.

"I remember that Christmas." Dad points to the picture.

"It was awful."

Mom gets up, picks up another gift, and joins us. "Those sessions …" Her voice cracks. "You pulled through. Mattie and you really got close that first year. I'm glad you met her."

The smile on my mom's face makes me all toasty inside. "You called us the Terrible Two."

She and my dad laugh.

Despite being sad about the dragon, I laugh too. I put the picture aside, take a breath, and look up at my mom and dad. "If I don't get my dragon, I don't want to do this again."

"Carmen," Mom says.

"It's too hard, and I hate the way the charms make me sick. I want to be able to enjoy eating like these last few days. If I don't get Rella, then I can't go through the process again. I get I was selected, but maybe I'm not meant to be a Dragon Keeper."

The tears in my mom's eyes force me to look at my dad.

"I'm too tired, Daddy." The color slowly drains from his normally warm face. "I can't do it anymore. I want to rest."

"Don't talk like that. You're going to get your dragon." My mom's voice is so loud I fall back into my pillow.

"I'm just saying if I don't get it, then I don't want to do it anymore. Two times is enough. Give someone else a chance." I don't want to hurt them, but I need them to understand.

"You're going to get your dragon." Dad's voice breaks, and for the first time, I see all the uncertainty and fear in his face he's been hiding from me.

"Okay." I'm not going to push it. I said what I wanted to say, and they heard me, but I can't push them. I want to make sure they understand it's okay. I don't need a dragon. If it isn't meant to be, then I have to be fine with that and so do my parents.

My mom bites at her lips and pushes another wrapped gift into my hands. "This is from Santa."

"But I didn't write a list." I glance at the box.

"I guess you've been good enough this year that he didn't need a letter or a list." My mom wipes her eyes.

I smile, realizing this is the very last Christmas I'm going to spend here no matter what happens. I take a breath and open the wrapping, and there in a new box is my own cell phone. I grin up at my folks. A warm tingle starts in my toes, and I adjust how I'm lying in bed. My stomach grumbles again, and I realize I haven't been this hungry since before I started my training. Maybe I am finally getting used to the charms.

No, that isn't it, something is different. I'm feeling different, feeling stronger. Then I sense it. It starts at the bottom of toes and rushes up through my body. I turn to the window. The box falls out of my hand, and I start crying.

"Carmen?" my dad says.

"*Mija*." My mother's hands tighten around me.

"I'm calling the doctor. Something's wrong." He reaches behind me.

"No," I gasp, "it's Rella." I point to the window. "Open the window." Outside the window in the rain is a Blue Bottom Dragon. She's tiny, barely the size of the cat. Her purple wings are flapping hard, and she is fighting to stay in the air. Rella is squawking and starting to hit the window with her muzzle to get into my room. Our eyes lock as she nips at the window, and I nod. It's real. She's real. I knew it all along.

"I got my dragon."

4

RELLA AND GARY FLAP AROUND above Mattie and me. Rella nips at Gary's tail, and he flips around midair and nosedives right at her, but Rella is lean and fast and easily dodges his attack. Mattie laughs, and I chuckle at them.

This has been the best Christmas ever. My first full Christmas with Rella. I've only had to come to the Dragon Training Campus four times this year—once a quarter to have them check on my bond with Rella and adjust my charms if needed. So far, I'm fine and so is Rella. This is my last check-in before it becomes twice a year.

I reach into my pocket and feel for my newest bonding charm. It's still there. This one smells of lavender. Not the awful rosemary-and-coffee one my dad gave me, or the not-so-bad-smelling cinnamon-and-vanilla one from my *abuela*.

"Are you going to be able to come to Reno for my thirteenth birthday?" Mattie pulls out her cell phone and checks a message.

We've been sitting out with the dragons all afternoon, and it's been nice, despite the chill in the air. I pull at my scarf and jacket, trying to keep the cold out.

"I want to. It depends on my parents, if they'll bring me." I pull out my cell as well to make a note about talking to my parents.

"You could take the train." Mattie nudges me. "It's only half a day."

I laugh. "Right. My parents let me go alone on the train ..." I shake my head. "It takes too long."

"You won't be alone." Mattie points to Rella.

"True, but I still don't think my parents will let me go."

Mattie frowns. I hate her frown. It hides her pretty blue eyes. This is only the second time we've seen each other this year. We've texted and Facetimed, but it's not the same.

"Well, try. Okay."

I nod. "You have my word."

•　　•　　•

I haven't seen Mattie in months, not since my *quinceañera*. Well, we saw each other at Jasper's funeral, but that was an awful day and I don't want to think about that. Not today. Getting off the train in downtown Reno is weird because the train station is all underground. But I find Mattie at once as she rushes over to me and we hug.

"I can't believe you made it."

"There was no way I was going to miss your sixteenth birthday." I adjust my backpack and catch a whiff of the lavender-and-rosemary charm. It's a new charm I got from the dragon center. I don't mind it as long as it helps me keep my bond with Rella.

"Coming down for your *quinceañera* was easy. It was summer, and my folks didn't mind getting rid of me."

We laugh.

"I know, right." I inhale her strawberry scent. I've missed it.

"Well, you're here and I'm here ..."

"And it's going to be great. You totally rock for having your party on Saturday."

"Anything for my girl." Mattie gives me a peck on the cheek. I tingle all over.

There is a screech above us as Rella bolts for Gary, and the two fly through the air, spinning together as they nip at each other. They are both getting so big. Rella is about as big as I am, and Gary is a little bigger than Mattie. Mattie and I chuckle. I take Mattie's hand in mine as we walk to her car.

This is going to be a great weekend.

•   •   •

"I thought you were going to come to school here?" I say to the screen, waiting for Mattie to respond. The plan was for her to transfer to San Jose State to their criminal justice program, now that I got accepted at Santa Clara University.

"Carmen, UNR has a really good program and transferring would be a pain in the ass." Mattie flips her hair over her shoulder. "Look, we can still see each other. It's not like you can't take the high-speed rail to Sacramento. Then jump on the train the rest of the way.

I can do the same thing. Or you could drive, but the train's faster."

I try not to frown, but it's too late. Mattie senses my disappointment. "I just ... I miss you and Rella misses Gary."

"I know. I miss you, too."

The truth is, I was hoping she would move down here and we could share an apartment. The dragons could spend time together, and we could both work on our degrees. With all the unanswered texts and the missed video chats, I shouldn't be surprised this is happening. Even as busy as I am, I still make time for her. I just wish she would do the same for me. My mom says it's because we're not kids anymore, but I have to wonder if maybe Mattie doesn't want to be with me anymore. Or possibly she met someone else. I don't know and I don't want to ask, because I don't want to fight again.

"Am I going to see you at Christmas?"

"Absolutely," Mattie says. "We're going to be at my folks' cabin in North Shore. You're coming up on the twenty-sixth, right?"

I nod.

There is no way I am going to miss Christmas with Mattie. It is the best time of year, especially since her parents bought the cabin a few years ago. The snow is wicked, and it's a nice break, especially from my crazy family. I swear Aunty Rebecca's only goal is to fatten me up with tamales, but as good as they are, I don't mind. It means I have to watch what I eat the rest of the time.

"Crap," Mattie says as her screen blinks. "I have to head to work. Call me this weekend, okay?" She kisses her hand, then touches it to the screen. "Love you."

"Love you, too." I kiss my hand, then do the same.

I sigh as the monitor goes blank. I pick up the vanilla-and-berry charm and toss it between my hands. I look over to Rella and she huffs. "Sorry, girl. You can see Gary next time."

•   •   •

I slam the door, causing Rella to start. "What the hell!" I can't believe Mattie would do this. I've been planning this trip for months. "We're not going to be around for Christmas." I mimic Mattie's voice in an unflattering way and pretend to flick my short brown hair over my shoulder like she does.

I've hardly seen her. She's barely around. Doesn't keep our dates and comes up with excuses not to see and talk to me. I'm sure she's seeing someone else, but she keeps denying it.

"What the hell is wrong with her?" I mumble under my breath.

I pull the vanilla-and-berry-scented charm from my neck and toss it on my dresser. I can't smell it right now.

There's a knock at the door.

"What?"

"Can I come in?" Mom's gentle voice barely makes it past the door.

I cross over to the door and open it, then fall into Rella's large frame for warmth and comfort. Rella is the size of my bed now, and it amazes me how she still fits in my room, but she does and I don't question it. After all, dragons are special creatures, and right now, my dragon is the only one who understands me. The only one who can really comfort me.

"I didn't mean to overhear," Mom says. "So, you're not going to Mattie's this Christmas?"

"We spend Christmas and New Year's together every year, for as long as I can remember." Rella's breath brushes past my ears.

"I know, *mija,* and I'm sorry." She rubs my back. "It doesn't make it any better, but your father and I are glad you'll be here. We can spend more time together. We love Mattie, but it's nice to have our daughter around." My mom rubs my shoulder.

I face her. "I just ..."

"I know, honey. I do. It was hard for me to be apart from your dad when we were dating." She chuckles. "Still is. Well, most days. But don't let it affect your relationship. Mattie cares about you."

"I'm not so sure. What if she met someone else?" I run my hand over Rella's belly, and a little puff of smoke escapes her nose. "What if this is her way of breaking up with me?"

"Oh, *mija,* don't say that."

"It's like she's pulling away from me, and I don't know why. Did I do something wrong?"

"Of course not." My mom forces me to turn and look at her. "You are a wonderful girl. You and Mattie are lucky to have each other."

"I don't feel so lucky."

"I know."

Tears tug at my eyes. "I just love her so much. Maybe I'm being too needy. What's wrong with me?"

"Nothing's wrong with you. Relationships are complicated." I hear the frown in her voice. At least she accepts who I am and realizes my relationship with Mattie—assuming I still have one—isn't some phase or side effect of the dragon training. "I've never seen two people more perfectly matched than you and Mattie."

"Sometimes I don't know, Mom." I sigh.

"There's always Rob. He's a good guy and likes you."

"Gross, we're friends, and he has a way-too-unhealthy affinity for Starbucks and Cup of Noodle Soup." I glare at her.

"Throwing it out there. You never know. A mother can hope." She rests a hand on my leg.

I shoot her another sore face.

"Anyway, I knew there was something special between you and Mattie. The moment you two met, you started telling everyone you were going to marry her. You never faltered, even when you wanted to give up on ..." She pointed to Rella.

"Maybe it's time. Maybe we ran our course." Tears dance in my eyes. "Mattie and I haven't seen each other nearly as much as we used to. She still won't move down here, and I'm still at SCU." I wipe at the tears that are falling down my cheek.

"*Mija*, don't make any rash choices." My mother gives me a big hug and whispers into my hair. "We love you no matter what."

"I know, Mom." I hug my mom really hard.

She leans back and brushes the loose hair back over my shoulder. She crosses over to exit my room and smiles. "It'll all work out." She opens the door and leaves.

I brush at my teary eyes. "What am I going to do?" I meet Rella's peaceful gaze and hug her tight.

●　　●　　●

I'm running down the hall of the new training center in Reno. I had to leave Rella outside. She is almost as big as a car now, so she can't come in, but she'll get over it. Maybe she can find Gary and figure out what is happening. I stop at the door, then rush in.

"Mattie," I say.

Mattie's lying in bed. Her eyes are closed. She is under the blanket. Various charms are all around her. My nose is assaulted with odd scents that I can't distinguish and that don't mix well together. The room is small, but Mattie has a window that looks out to the falling snow.

How could this be happening at Christmas?

"What happened?"

Her mom stands and hugs me. "Oh, Carmen, it happened so fast. One minute, she was fine, helping me make Christmas cookies, and the next, she passed out. Oh, honey."

"The Master Dragon Trainer says that the bond with Gary is breaking down. We knew this could happen, there would always be a chance of their bond deteriorating, but she's been healthy for so long, we never thought there would be a relapse, not like this," her father says. "We've been trying all these new dragon-bonding charms, but nothing seems to be working."

It's like Jasper all over again. Even with Gary still here. Mattie can't die, not like Jasper did when we were teenagers.

"My dad is going to come up tomorrow. He and his students have been working on some new bonding charms." I nod. "They'll work. He'll make sure that Mattie and Gary's bond is strong again so they can fight off the curse together."

"I hope so," her mom says and steps back, glancing down at Mattie.

Her glasses are on the side table, and her pretty brown hair is a mess. I want to grab a brush and put her hair in a ponytail for her.

Later.

All the fights and drama fade from my memory. It was all so dumb and petty. It doesn't matter that I haven't seen her in half a year. I'm here now.

"Hi, Carmen," Mattie whispers. Her blue eyes blink open, and a smile blooms across her lips. "I thought I heard your voice."

I cross to the bed and take her hand. "You know I'd be here for you."

"I'm glad. I was worried that I wouldn't get to see you, before ..."

"Hush now. Don't think like that. They're going to see what kind of curse is affecting you and why your bond with Gary is failing, and my dad and the Master Dragon Trainer are going to come up with the perfect charm. Your link with Gary will be stronger than ever."

"You promise?"

"Of course. Rella told me so." I give her hand a squeeze.

Mattie laughs, then starts to cough.

"I should have gone into magic like my dad wanted ..." I rub Mattie's hand. "I could have helped."

"You sucked at magic and you know it," Mattie says with the ghost of a snicker. "You're going to be an amazing computer engineer, just like your mom."

"But that can't help you."

"You being here helps me. I've missed you. I've been so busy with school and work I hardly have any time for anything these days."

I want to kick myself for the stupid fight. Not talking for months and now here I am. Mattie's curse has returned, her bond with Gary is in jeopardy, and I wasted all that time. Never again. I'm not going to waste any more time.

I get a flash of blue and green at the window, but with the snow, I don't see it anymore. I hope Rella is giving Gary all kinds of hell for this. I know it's not his fault. It's the bond and the charms, but still. Gary has been with Mattie for eleven years, and bonds shouldn't weaken after this long. I know they sometimes do, and it can happen, but I never thought it would happen to Mattie. Never. She was always the more resilient of the two of us. Even when I wanted to give up, she made me want to fight. Now I need to do that for her.

The door opens, and the facility's Master Dragon Trainer walks in. She's young with cocoa-colored skin and pretty full lips. I stand.

"MDT Simpson, this is Mattie's girlfriend, Carmen," Mattie's father says.

"I've heard a lot about you, Carmen. I'm looking forward to meeting your father tomorrow. It'll be good to have someone with his experience and talent around."

"Thank you." I wring my hands. I'm scared to ask, but I have to know. "You don't think this happened because Rella and Gary haven't seen each other in a while, do you?"

The Master Dragon Trainer smiles at me. "Of course not. That isn't how these things work. Sometimes, over time the bonds and the charms break down. Or the body develops a resistance to the treatment. Unfortunately, it can be any number of things. Even with all the advances we've made, nothing is 100 percent."

I nod. "I understand." That is what happened to Jasper. The curse was too much for him, and with no dragon to help him fight, there wasn't much of anything anyone could do. Even with the fancy expensive charms his parents tried.

"Now, Mattie, we're going to run a few additional tests, but I don't want you to worry. We're going to take really good care of you. I can assure you we'll be doing everything we can to get you healthy again."

Mattie smiles.

I wink at her, trying to hide my fear and worry. I hope it works.

•　　　•　　　•

The snow blows outside the cabin window as I roll my cup of cocoa in my hands. It's hard to believe today is the day.

I think back to Mattie in the training facility. Her road to recovery was a long one. Master Dragon Trainer Simpson and my dad had to work for months to test the new magical charms on Mattie. At least she didn't lose her hair, and when they finished, the new charm worked. Mattie and Gary were in sync, and their bond was strong and stable. With Gary by her side, Mattie was able to fight off the curse again, and there haven't been any signs of a return.

Once she was healthy again, she returned to school and finished off her degree. Seeing Mattie get her diploma was amazing. Part of me felt guilty because I was able to graduate sooner, but right now, it doesn't matter.

A smile glides over my lips as I see a flash of color outside as Gary and Rella play in the snow.

Those two are crazy. It's freezing out there.

When I told my folks what my plan was for this Christmas, they were both honestly thrilled for me. I suppose they weren't surprised—no one really will be, well, except for Mattie. She might be.

I finish off my cocoa and get up, leaving my view of the white snow as it floats from the sky. I drop my half-full cup off in the sink and put together the breakfast I've made. Checking the tray, I pull the plate from the oven. On the red-and-green dish are all of Mattie's favorites—eggs, bacon, and toast—I place it next to the cup of hot cocoa and make my way to the bedroom.

"Merry Christmas," I say as I peek through the door and bring the tray over and place it on the side of the bed.

Mattie rolls over on her side and takes a pillow and covers her head of messy brown hair. "What time is it?"

"Time to wake up and have breakfast. I cooked."

"Ugh ... do I have to?"

I huff. "Well, if you don't, then you don't get your present."

"That's blackmail."

"Possibly, but that's how it works."

Mattie tosses the pillow to the side and finally opens her eyes, blinks several times at me, then looks at the tray. "What's going on?" Her gaze narrows on me.

"Nothing. I'm just basking in the glow that is Mattie."

Mattie crosses her blue eyes, squishes her nose, and sticks out her tongue.

I chuckle.

Mattie sits up and takes the tray. "Looks good." She sniffs it. "Smells good too."

"Thank you."

I sit on the bed and enjoy this quiet moment as Mattie eats her breakfast. The snow continues to fall outside the window. Everything is covered in a blanket of white. It's hard to make out any of the trees or the mountains in the distance. If it keeps falling at this rate, we're going to be snowed in. Which is fine with me. There is another flash of the dragons outside. I doubt they'll mind either. I snatch a piece of Mattie's bacon off her plate. I wasn't able to eat earlier, but the bacon smells too good to pass up.

Mattie leans back, sipping her cocoa. "My compliments to the chief." She wipes her mouth with the napkin.

I smile. Within one tick of the clock, my mouth is like a desert and my heart is pounding in my chest. I thought this would be a lot easier. I had this whole speech planned, and now I can barely speak. I glance around for a glass of water or something, but I left my cocoa in the kitchen and Mattie is drinking hers.

Ugh.

"What's wrong? You've been acting strange this whole trip."

I do my best to clear my throat and pull out a small box. "Merry Christmas." My voice cracks, and I'm forced to clear my throat again.

"What's this?"

I go to speak, but no words come. I nod at the box.

Mattie opens the gift, and a gentle gasp leaves her lips.

With great effort, words exit my mouth. "I've been waiting since I was eleven years old to ask you. There is no one I love more in this world than you, and there is no one I want to spend my life with more than you. Will you … ah … marry me?"

Mattie's blue eyes sparkle with tears as she slips the ring out of the box. "You already know my answer."

• • •

"Honey, you need to stop pacing."

Mom's no help. She's sitting in her chair, her right leg bouncing off the knee of her left leg like there's no tomorrow. Her black hair is all pulled up off her face in a French braid. She had it colored to hide all the gray, and she looks beautiful. I can't tell which one of us is more nervous, even though she's trying to play it cool.

"I can't help it." I tug at my dress. I have blue and purple ribbons in my hair that are starting to annoy the hell out of me. I can't believe I thought it was a cute idea.

The door opens to the dressing room. My dad walks in. His brown hair is now mostly gray, but he still has his dimples. I remember him being so tall, and now we're almost eye to eye, especially when I wear heels. Like today.

He takes both my hands. "You look beautiful."

"Thanks, Dad."

He kisses my cheek. "Are you ready?"

I nod. "What about Rella and Gary?"

"They're all settled," my dad reassures me.

I take in the changing room. It's small with just the basics. A few chairs, a full-length mirror, and a desk-table thing. My street clothes are hanging on a makeshift clothes rack. Makeup and brushes everywhere. It's a mess, but I'm here. I'm finally here.

"Okay." I take a deep breath and reach out my hand to my mom. The three of us stand there, and I smile at them. "Thank you for everything. I know what it took for me to get here. You're the best parents, and I'm sorry for all the trouble I caused you."

My mom starts waving her hand in front of her face. "Don't make me cry. The holographer and his assistant will kill me if I have puffy eyes."

"I knew from the time we found out," my dad says, "you would beat it."

I chuckle. The thought of being a Dragon Keeper warms my heart.

"Now look at you. You finished college; you're getting married; you're doing all the things you ever wanted. You never gave up." He kisses my cheek.

But I wanted to give up. When I was eleven, right before I got Rella, I wanted to give in to the curse. I didn't want to fight anymore. Then when Mattie was cursed again, I didn't want to go on without her. I know there were curses knocking at my door then, and I almost answered. Even Rella sensed I wanted to give up. But I didn't. I fought. The dragons can only do so much. I had to do the rest. Magic would never be 100 percent.

"Let's do this," I say, and we head out.

•   •   •

I'm the first at the altar, which is fine with me. The sooner we get this over with, the faster we can get to the party and the wine, even though I'm not supposed to have wine. It reacts badly with my bonding charms. But both Mattie and I get to splurge today. The other reason I don't mind being up here first is I get to watch Mattie walk down the aisle. I've waited eighteen years for this moment, and I don't want to miss it.

The church is decorated in red and green for the Christmas holiday, and I'm happy that we get to have a Christmas wedding. This time of year means the most to me. So many milestones were reached. Mattie and I became friends during that first Christmas at the center. We had our first kiss the Christmas I was fourteen. We got engaged the Christmas we were up at her parents' cabin in North Shore, the year after our scare with Mattie's curse returning. We got snowed in, and it was perfect. Christmas was also when I got my dragon.

I peek over to where Rella and Gary are sitting. They are being so well-behaved, and they're happy. Their tails are intertwined. We—no, I owe this moment to them.

The music begins, and Mattie crosses the entry with both her mother and father, then walks down the aisle. She's beautiful in her gown. It's not red and green but cream, and it hugs her curves perfectly. Her blue eyes sparkle in the light, and her brown hair is pinned up with simple braids.

I take a breath and face my folks. My dad holds up a small bag, one of his charms. I have the same one tucked into my dress. Ever since I almost lost Mattie, I'm never without my bonding charms, not even for a second. I can't help but smile. I have to look away, or I'll laugh.

I face Mattie. My Mattie, as she walks closer. She's the most beautiful woman I've ever seen. I turn away because I don't want to cry. Rella and Gary huff, and small puffs of smoke come out of their noses. They seem so small now, but they're not. They are mighty dragons and always will be.

I've been a Dragon Keeper since I was eleven, and I will continue to be one. It won't be easy, and some people, even after years and years, lose their dragons. That won't happen to me. My family sacrificed too much. I went through too much to get here. I won't allow it. And as long as I have Mattie, my beautiful Mattie, with me, I can do anything. We can do anything, together.

I take a deep breath, and I get a whiff of strawberries.

A hand slips into mine. It's Mattie. She smiles at me and whispers, "I got my dragon for Christmas."

About the Author

M.D. Neu is an international award-winning inclusive queer Fiction Writer with a love for writing and travel. Living in the heart of Silicon Valley, and growing up around technology, he's always been fascinated with what could be. When M.D. Neu isn't writing, he works for a non-profit and travels with his biggest supporter and his harshest critic, Eric, his husband of twenty plus years.

Also by the Author

THE REUNION

M.D. Neu

It's been 20 years since the quiet Midwestern town of Lakeview was struck by tragedy.

Available in trade paperback and digital editions from
Water Dragon Publishing
waterdragonpublishing.com

You Might Also Enjoy

ONE FOR THE ROAD

Melissa M. Buhl & and Brian C. E. Buhl

When Father Time goes missing, it's up to Tina and Akexa to use their wits and their magic to bring him in. If Father Time isn't there for the New Year's ritual, it will be certain doom for the entire city.

Available in hardcover, trade paperback,
and digital editions from
Water Dragon Publishing
waterdragonpublishing.com

www.ingramcontent.com/pod-product-compliance
Lightning Source LLC
Chambersburg PA
CBHW071207300726
48975CB00004B/1313